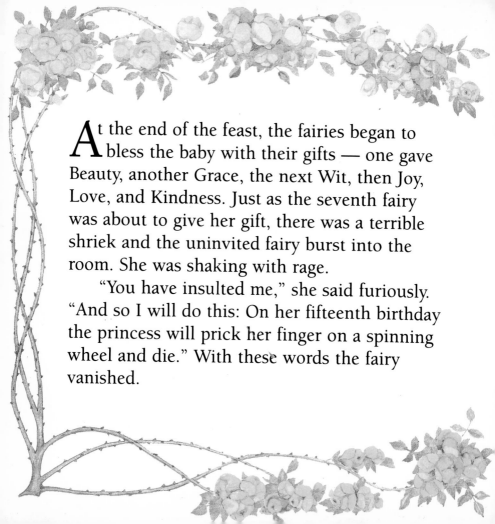

At the end of the feast, the fairies began to bless the baby with their gifts — one gave Beauty, another Grace, the next Wit, then Joy, Love, and Kindness. Just as the seventh fairy was about to give her gift, there was a terrible shriek and the uninvited fairy burst into the room. She was shaking with rage.

"You have insulted me," she said furiously. "And so I will do this: On her fifteenth birthday the princess will prick her finger on a spinning wheel and die." With these words the fairy vanished.

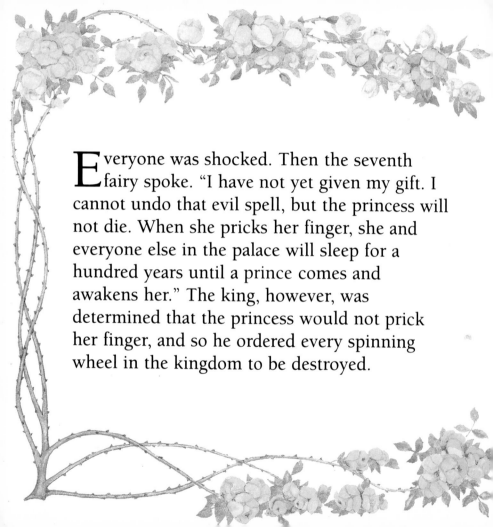

Everyone was shocked. Then the seventh fairy spoke. "I have not yet given my gift. I cannot undo that evil spell, but the princess will not die. When she pricks her finger, she and everyone else in the palace will sleep for a hundred years until a prince comes and awakens her." The king, however, was determined that the princess would not prick her finger, and so he ordered every spinning wheel in the kingdom to be destroyed.

The child grew to be beautiful, kind, and happy. On her fifteenth birthday, as she was strolling about the palace, she came to a little garret she had never seen before at the top of the tower. An old woman was spinning at a wheel, and the princess asked if she could try. But as she reached out to the spindle, she pricked her finger and immediately fell into a deep sleep — as did everyone else in the palace! The fairy who had saved the princess's life had her placed upon a canopied bed in the finest room in the palace. The princess looked as lovely as ever, yet her eyes remained shut.

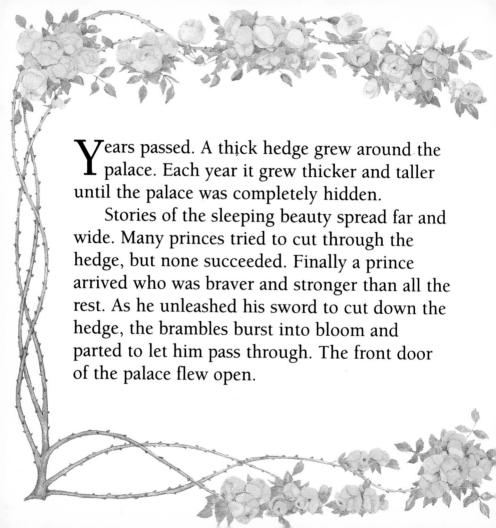

Years passed. A thick hedge grew around the palace. Each year it grew thicker and taller until the palace was completely hidden.

Stories of the sleeping beauty spread far and wide. Many princes tried to cut through the hedge, but none succeeded. Finally a prince arrived who was braver and stronger than all the rest. As he unleashed his sword to cut down the hedge, the brambles burst into bloom and parted to let him pass through. The front door of the palace flew open.

When the prince entered the princess's chamber, he was so taken by her beauty that he fell upon his knees trembling beside the bed. Then he kissed her cheek and the princess awoke. "It is you, my prince," she said.

Suddenly the palace came to life. When the king and queen found their daughter with the prince, they were elated. The prince and princess married and lived happily ever after.

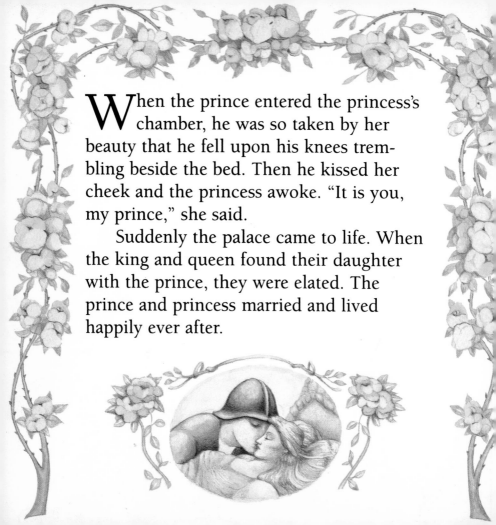